TOMMY NINER

AND THE
PLANET OF
DANGER

ALSO BY TONY BRADMAN IN HAPPY CAT BOOKS

TOMMY NINER AND THE
MOON OF DOOM

TOMMY NINER AND
THE MYSTERY SPACESHIP

AND THE
PLANET OF
DANGER

Tony Bradman

Illustrated by Martin Chatterton

HAPPY CAT BOOKS

Published by
Happy Cat Books
An imprint of Catnip Publishing Ltd
Islington Business Centre
3-5 Islington High Street
London N1 9LQ

This edition first published 2007
1 3 5 7 9 10 8 6 4 2

Copyright © Tony Bradman, 2007
Illustrations © Martin Chatterton, 2007

The moral right of the author and illustrator has been asserted

A CIP catalogue record for this book is available from the British Library

ISBN   978-1-905117-41-3

Printed in Poland

www.catnippublishing.co.uk

CONTENTS

1 THE MYSTERY SIGNAL

Tommy Niner sat at the controls of the Stardust, the spaceship that was his home. He listened to its engines humming steadily. On the screen in front of him, stars zoomed past.

He had been on watch for hours, and he was bored stiff.

"Anything to report, Ada?" he said. There was no reply.

"Ada, you haven't dozed off, have you?"

I never fall asleep on duty.

"Er . . . what, me?" said a voice. It belonged to someone who had obviously just woken up with a start.

Tommy smiled. Ada was the ship's computer. She was an old model, and Grandad was always saying she should have been replaced years ago. Ada said much the same about him.

"Never mind, Ada," said Tommy. "I don't blame you. If only something *exciting* would happen. This is the most boring patrol we've ever been on."

When the Galactic Council had ordered them to find out why spaceships kept going missing in Sector 13, Tommy had thought it would be an interesting, maybe even dangerous, mission. But they had been patrolling for days, and so far they hadn't come across anything unusual at all.

"If you ask me, we might as well go back to base," said Ada. "There's nothing here but empty space . . . Wait a minute, though. I do believe I'm

Beep!
Beep!
Beep!
picking up a signal."

"Ha, ha, very funny, Ada," said Tommy, yawning. "Pull the other one. It's got asteroids on."

"I'm not joking, Tommy,' said Ada seriously. "I really *am* picking up a signal."

"What sort of signal?" said Tommy, leaning forward. Perhaps things were beginning to look up.

"I don't know," said Ada. "It's familiar, but I can't quite place it. My memory's not what it used to be, I'm afraid. Anyway, it sounds . . . well, sort of urgent."

"Wow! I'd better call Dad."

"What is it, Thomas?" Commander Niner's grumpy voice boomed into the control deck. "Your orders

3

were not to bother me unless it was for something urgent. You know this is supposed to be my rest period."

"I'm sorry, Dad, but –"

"Anyway, I'm not very happy with you, my lad. I've told you before how important it is to keep a spaceship's cabins neat and clean. Yours is an absolute disgrace. When was the last time you tidied it, eh? Can you tell me that?"

"Well, I –"

"Exactly. You can't, can you? I found a mug under your bed that's probably been there for a week. Mind you, your cabin isn't as bad as Grandad's. If he makes any more of his crazy machines there won't be room for him."

Tommy sighed. He had heard it all before.

Hardly a day went by without

Grandad announcing he'd devised some amazing new machine. The trouble was that none of them ever seemed to work properly. Tommy had lost count of the number of times Grandad had nearly blown himself up.

"Dad, will you just listen?" Tommy said. "Ada's picking up a signal, and she thinks it sounds urgent."

"Well, why didn't you tell me that in the first place?" said Dad.

"But you —" Tommy started to say. Dad didn't let him finish.

"I don't want any more of your excuses, Thomas," he said. "I'm on my way. And as soon as we've sorted out this signal business, you're to tidy your cabin. Understood?"

"Aye, aye, sir!" said Tommy smartly.
Then he stuck his tongue out at the
intercom.

②RED ALERT!

A few moments later the door opened
and Dad came in. He sat down and put
a mug on the control panel. It must be
the one from my cabin, thought Tommy.

"Now, what sort of signal is it, Ada?"
said Dad.

"I'm trying
to find out,
Commander," said
Ada. "I've been
through most of my
information banks,
but I still don't recognize it."

"Where's it coming from,
then?" said Dad.

"I'm not too sure," said
Ada.

"Somewhere up ahead, I think."

"Well, you're a lot of help, aren't you?" said Dad crossly. "Is there *anything* you can tell me about it? Or would that be too much to ask?"

"There's no need to lose your temper, Commander," said Ada in a snooty voice. "I *am* doing my best. And it would be much easier if I wasn't missing half my energy cells."

"They were all there yesterday," said Dad, sounding puzzled. "I checked them myself. I don't understand where they could have gone . . ." Then his face changed. "Don't tell me. I think I can guess," he muttered. "Own up, Ada. Grandad took them, didn't he?"

"I told him you wouldn't like it," said Ada. "But he promised he'd put them back before you'd even notice they were gone."

"Oh, did he?" said Dad. "I'll have a
few words to say to him about that."

Just then the door opened again,
and Grandad himself arrived with a
triumphant smile on his face.

Tommy noticed he was carrying
an odd-looking box. It was covered in
switches and winking
lights.

"I will if I ever
meet him," said Dad.

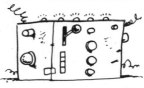

He pointed at Grandad's box. "Is that where Ada's energy cells went?"

"Ah," said Grandad. "I should have known that ancient calculator would never be able to keep quiet."

"Why, you scrawny old —" Ada started off, but a burst of electronic crackling drowned out the rest of her words.

"Temper, temper," said Grandad. "Anyway, I haven't come here to argue. I just wanted to show you how my new machine works."

"Not now, Grandad," said Dad. "Can't you see we're busy? Ada, what was all that noise?"

"The signal suddenly got a lot stronger, Commander," said Ada. She seemed very pleased with herself. "And I've just remembered what it is. No wonder I thought it sounded urgent. It's an SOS."

"It's a *what?*" shouted Dad.

Galloping galaxies! Hit the red alert button, Thomas!

"Aye, aye, sir!" said Tommy. But Grandad was in the way.

"This is my best invention yet," he was saying. "You see that mug? With this machine I can send it anywhere in the universe."

Dad was too busy concentrating on the control panel to listen to Grandad. Then Tommy noticed Dad was reaching forward to move the mug out of the way of some switches.

"Dad," said Tommy, "if I were you —"

"Right," said Grandad, turning a dial. "Here we go!"

A ray of light shot out of the box. There was a throbbing noise, then a bang, and the light vanished. When the smoke cleared, Grandad started hopping up and down with an even bigger smile on his face.

"You see, I told you it would work!" he was saying. Then his expression changed. "Oh dear," he said. "That wasn't supposed to happen."

The mug had disappeared. But so had Dad!

THE SEARCH BEGINS

"You've really done it this time, Grandad," said Tommy. "He'll be absolutely furious unless you get him back right away. You *can* get him back, can't you?"

Grandad reached into the box and pulled out a clump of frizzled, smoking wires.

"We might have a problem there, Tommy," he said. "I think it's going to take me a while to fix this."

"Oh, that's terrific, Grandad," said Tommy. "And I'll bet you don't even know where he's gone, do you?"

"Well, er, no," said Grandad. Then he smiled. "But don't worry, Tommy. I'm sure we'll find him."

Tommy wasn't so sure. He looked at the screen, which still showed nothing but stars. The universe was a very big place, and Dad might be anywhere. Tommy knew they could search for millions of years and never find him.

He wasn't even wearing a spacesuit.

Then Tommy had an idea.

"Ada," he said. "Do *you* know where he went?"

"I can't understand why you bother with that worn-out old heap," whispered Grandad. "I've met microwave ovens with more brains."

"I heard that," snapped Ada. "I wouldn't be so tired if you hadn't stolen my energy cells. And actually, I *did* manage to track Commander Niner for a while, so there."

Ada blew an electronic raspberry.

"Calm down, Ada," said Tommy. "You'll get your circuits in a twist. Just tell us where he is."

"I don't know *exactly*," said Ada. "But he was definitely heading for the star system that's coming up."

Tommy looked at the screen again. One star was now much bigger than the rest. As he watched, seven or eight planets came into view. Each one seemed to have several moons.

Suddenly Tommy felt very depressed.

"Can't you narrow it down a bit more?" he said.

"Not much," said Ada. "I can tell you

something else, though. The SOS was coming from somewhere in there, too."

"That's a coincidence," said Tommy.

As he said these words, Tommy wondered whether it was. But then, strange things often happen in space, he thought.

"It seems to have stopped now, though," said Ada. "I can't pick it up at all. Do you want me to keep trying?"

"No, Ada, finding Dad has got to come first," said Tommy. "We'll start with that big orange planet as it's the nearest. Is that all right with you, Grandad?"

"I beg your pardon?" said Grandad. He was fiddling with his broken machine. "You're in charge, Tommy."

"You could make an effort to sound a bit more interested, Grandad," said Tommy.

"Oh, right," said Grandad, trying to look concerned. But his eyes kept drifting back to his machine.

"OK, Ada," said Tommy with a sigh. "Full speed ahead. Let me know the second you find anything. And don't doze off."

"I won't," said Ada. "Cross my silicon chip and hope to die."

Tommy pressed some switches. He heard the booster rockets fire and felt the Stardust shift its course. Soon they were well on their way towards the orange planet. As they got closer, Tommy could see it had rings, like Saturn.

A little while later, he noticed something odd. A small grey dot had appeared on the screen. It grew larger, and larger, and larger, then started to break up into a cloud of smaller dots.

Suddenly Tommy realized what it was.

 4 METEOR STORM

"What?" said Ada. She sounded startled. "There's no need to shout, Tommy. I wasn't *really* asleep. Is there something you'd like me to do?"

"How about making sure none of those meteors hits us?" said Tommy. "They look very big."

"Actually, I don't think I can," said Ada. "They're moving too fast."

"I told you she was useless," said Grandad.

"That's a good one coming from *you*," said Ada.

"This is no time to start bickering," said Tommy quickly.

A row of lights began flashing on the

Give me laser power, Ada, and make it snappy. Somebody had better try and save us.

control panel, and two objects rose out of it. They were shaped like gun handles, and each had a large button on the side. Tommy took hold of them and leaned back in his seat.

He was just in time. The huge grey mass of a meteor almost filled the screen. Tommy aimed carefully at its middle, then pressed both buttons. A

blinding laser beam zapped out, and the
meteor was blown into tiny pieces.

"Well done, Tommy!" shouted
Grandad. "But look out, here comes
another!"

Tommy blasted that meteor, and

the next one, and the one after

that. He kept shooting until the

Stardust was safely through.

24

"Phew," he said. "I didn't think we were going to make it."

"We won't," said Ada. "Not if we stick to this course, anyway. There's another lot coming straight for us."

"Oh no," said Tommy. "I'll never hit all those! Ada, get us out of here!"

"I'm trying to," said Ada, "but I'm picking up meteors everywhere. In fact, there's only one direction open to us. Do you think we should go that way, Tommy?"

"Don't be stupid, Ada!" shouted Tommy, his eyes fixed on the spaceship-sized rock hurtling towards them. "Of course we should!"

The Stardust swung sharply round. The meteor tumbled past harmlessly, and Tommy breathed a sigh of relief.

A new planet appeared on the screen almost immediately. It was a very nasty shade of green, with dashes of sickly

yellow. Tommy wondered whether Dad was down there.

I hope not, he thought. Just looking at the place made Tommy uneasy. He couldn't explain it, but the closer they got, the more he felt as if something was watching them, something evil . . .

Then Tommy realized they were approaching the green planet a little too quickly.

"Aren't we going a bit fast, Ada?" he said.

"Yes, Tommy," said Ada. "That's because of the gravity beam."

"Gravity beam?" said Tommy. "What are you talking about now, Ada?"

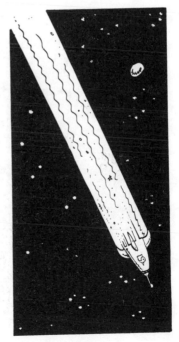

"Oh, didn't I tell you?" she said. "A powerful beam is dragging us towards the green planet. We don't seem to be able to break free of it, either."

"What does that mean?" said Tommy, with a sinking feeling.

"Really, Tommy," said Ada. "You're a bright boy. I thought you'd have understood that it means we're going to crash. In exactly sixteen seconds, actually."

No, fifteen, fourteen, thirteen, twelve, eleven...

CRASH LANDING!

...ten, nine, eight...

"Don't just sit there counting, Ada!" shouted Tommy. "*Do* something, for heaven's sake!"

The Stardust was screaming down towards the surface of the planet. All Tommy could see on the screen now was a fiery red glow. The control deck had quickly become very warm.

"I'm sorry, Tommy," said Ada. "There's nothing I can do. No, wait a minute, something has just occurred to me."

29

"It had better be good," said Tommy.

"I could warn you to brace yourself," said Ada.

"Thanks a lot," said Tommy. "I'd thought of that already."

"Oh well, that's all right then," said Ada. "I'll resume the countdown."

Tommy closed his eyes and waited for the explosion.

one...ZERO!

But the explosion never came. Instead, the Stardust suddenly levelled out. They flew along for a few seconds, then Tommy felt the ship dip down. There was a tremendous bang as its base hit the ground.

They slid forward with a terrible screeching of metal. Then

Tommy was thrown from his seat as they came to rest with a final lurch.

Suddenly it was very quiet. Tommy lay dazed on the floor, amazed he was still alive. Then he heard a groan.

"Grandad!" he said. "Where are you?"

"Over here, Tommy," said a muffled voice. But Tommy couldn't see anyone.

The control deck was in a shocking mess. The whole thing was tilted to one side. Wires hung loose, and sparks leapt from some of the panels. Cupboards had flown open in the crash, and everything inside them had fallen out.

It took a long time, but Tommy found Grandad at last, under a pile of spacesuits.

"Are you OK, Grandad?" he said, brushing him down.

"Yes, Tommy," said Grandad with a weak smile. He was still holding his

machine. "I'm fine."

"I doubt that," said Ada. "I'll bet he's as mad as ever, unless our bumpy landing has knocked some sense into him."

"It was a bit more than bumpy, Ada," said Tommy. Grandad just glared at her. "You'd better give us a damage report."

What do you want first? The good news or the bad news?

"I could do without the jokes, Ada,"
sighed Tommy. For some reason he was
finding it hard to stay patient. "Just tell
us the worst."

"We've got a broken tail light, a lot
of dents and scratches, and we've lost
all our aerials. But the *really* bad news is
that the ship's engines are wrecked."

"Can we repair them?" said Tommy.

"Not without a lot of spare parts,"
said Ada. "And I haven't the *faintest* idea
where we're going to get those."

The meaning of Ada's words sank
into Tommy's shell-shocked mind.

"Are you telling us we're trapped
here?" he said.

That's right, Tommy. Probably for ever.

6 Strange New World

Tommy sat with his head in his hands. Ada and Grandad were arguing.

"No, you silly old fool, we can't call for help," Ada was saying. "The radio is broken, too."

"No problem," said Grandad. "I'll mend it."

"Don't make me laugh," said Ada. "You couldn't mend —"

"Excuse me," interrupted Tommy, "but can I get a word in? You said there was some good news, Ada. What is it?"

"Oh yes, I'd quite forgotten," said Ada. "Well, I'm glad to say my scanners are working, and I've found Commander Niner. He's precisely three kilometres north of here."

Come on, Tommy. What are we waiting for?

"Hang on a second, Grandad," said Tommy. "Don't you think this is a bit peculiar? First we get a mystery SOS from this direction, then we're dragged down by a gravity beam. Someone seems pretty determined to get us here."

"It does sound like that, doesn't it?" said Grandad. "What are we going to do?"

"First things first," said Tommy. "I want to know more about this planet before I go for a walk on it. Give me a full scan, please, Ada."

"Sorry, Tommy, but I'm not strong enough for that," said Ada. "Of course, if I had all my energy cells . . ."

Tommy turned to give Grandad a nasty look. But Grandad was suddenly busy with his machine again.

"Oh well, we'll just have to do it the risky way," said Tommy. "Right, Grandad, let's get into our spacesuits. And I don't know about you, but I'm taking my blaster."

Ten minutes later, Tommy and Grandad were standing in the Stardust's main airlock.

"OK, Ada," said Tommy. "You can open up now."

Tommy had no idea what this strange new world would look like. It came as quite a surprise.

In front of him was a wall of enormous, weird-looking trees. They were part of a jungle which stretched as far as he could see. In the distance was a yellow mountain, and something below it shining in the bright sunlight.

Tommy took a small tracking device from the tool kit on his belt. It lit up and started bleeping softly when he pointed it at the mountain.

"Dad should be in that direction," he said, and set off.

"Hey, wait for me!" said Grandad. "I think

we'd better stick together. This place is really spooky."

Tommy knew exactly what he meant. That sense of being watched by something evil was even stronger now. And Tommy could feel it growing as they pushed through the dark, silent jungle.

"What was that?" Grandad whispered as they came into a big clearing.

"I didn't hear anything," said Tommy, trying to sound as if he wasn't worried. "You're just a bit jumpy, Grandad, that's all."

"There it is again," said Grandad, gripping Tommy's arm. "A sort of rustling. I don't like this, Tommy."

"Don't panic, Grandad," Tommy said.

But then Tommy saw something that made him want to panic, too.

A large creature was lumbering towards them out of the jungle. And it had the biggest claws Tommy had ever seen!

ROBOT ATTACK!

The creature looked like a giant spider that had been put together in a junk yard. It made a grinding, clanking noise as it moved. Between the claws, two beady red eyes stared at them.

"It's a robot!" said Tommy. He started to back away slowly, but Grandad stayed where he was.

"You're right, Tommy," he said, an expression of wonder on his face. "And what a magnificent machine it is, too! Don't worry, I'm sure it's friendly."

"It doesn't look very friendly to me," said Tommy. "And I'd rather not hang around to find out which of us is right."

Come on, Grandad – last one back to the Stardust is a wally!

"Wait a minute, Tommy. I'm sure I can talk to it," said Grandad. He held his hand up in the universal greeting. "Hail, mighty machine," he said. "We come to your planet in peace ..."

Grandad gave Tommy an "I-told-you-so" smile as the robot spider came to a sudden halt.

But it didn't talk back.

Instead, it gave off a high-pitched buzzing, and fired two dazzling beams from its eyes. They were aimed at

Tommy first, but moved quickly to Grandad and stayed on him.

For several seconds Grandad was bathed in a pool of red light. The buzzing grew even louder. Then, almost

as suddenly as they'd started, the beams
were turned off.

The robot spider began to come
forward once more. But now it was
moving a lot faster, and its claws
were snapping at them with a vicious
clacking sound.

"That's brilliant,
Grandad," said
Tommy. "You've
made it angry.
Have you got any
other good ideas?"

"Er, maybe we *should* go back to
the Stardust for a while," said Grandad
nervously. "The locals do seem a little
irritable."

They turned to run, but stopped dead
in their tracks. Coming towards them
from the other side of the clearing was a
second robot spider. They turned again,

only to see a third robot, and then a
fourth.

They were surrounded.

"I know I said I wanted more
excitement," said Tommy, "but this is
getting ridiculous." He pulled out his
blaster. "It looks as if we'll have to fight
them off, Grandad."

"I'm sorry, Tommy," said Grandad,
"but I think you'll be doing most of

the fighting. My blaster hasn't got an energy cell at the moment. I used it in my latest invention."

"I should have known," groaned Tommy.

The first robot spider was almost on top of them. Tommy raised his blaster and fired at its legs. But even though he blew one off, the spider kept coming. He whirled round and fired at the other

machines, but he couldn't stop them, either.

"It's no good, Grandad!" he shouted. "We're done for!"

Tommy expected the machines to rip them both to pieces with their claws. But they didn't. Instead, all four machines stopped at exactly the same instant. Red beams leapt from their eyes and focused on Grandad. Then some sort of rope snaked from the belly of one and wrapped itself tightly around him.

The machines started moving again . . . but now they were going backwards, out of the clearing! Tommy watched helplessly

as Grandad was dragged away. He fired
again and again at the robot spider
that had Grandad in its grip, but it was
useless.

Run for it,
Tommy! Save
yourself!

But the robot spiders obviously
weren't interested in Tommy. He put the
blaster in its holster. Silence flowed back
into the alien clearing.

Tommy Niner felt very, very alone.

⑧ Tommy Goes Exploring

Tommy thought about chasing the robot spiders, but decided against it.

If only Dad was here. He'd know what to do.

Then Tommy suddenly remembered Dad wasn't far away, according to Ada, at least. If he could find Dad, together they might be able to save Grandad.

BLEEP!

Tommy pulled out the tracking device.

The bleeping was much louder now, especially when he pointed the device in one direction – the part of the jungle into which Grandad had been dragged.

"There's no getting out of it, then," said Tommy grimly.

He walked over to the edge of the clearing. Standing there for a while, he screwed up his courage. Then he swallowed hard, and stepped into the jungle again.

The first thing he noticed was the destruction left by the robot spider. It must have gone in a perfectly straight line, knocking over any trees in its way.

Tommy checked the tracking device once more, although somehow he knew what it would tell him. The robot spider's trail would lead him to Dad, as well as to Grandad.

"Now that's what I call one

coincidence too many," said Tommy. "There *must* be something funny going on."

As he ran, Tommy thought about the robot spiders. Why had they only been interested in Grandad? Those red beams must have been scanning rays of some sort. What had they been looking for? Tommy racked his brains, but he couldn't work it out.

After a few minutes, Tommy stopped to get his breath back. He looked up the trail, and noticed there was more daylight ahead. That probably meant another clearing.

Tommy went forward carefully,

dodging from tree
to tree. He reached
the edge of the
jungle and looked
out.

What he saw made his eyes go as
wide as super-novas.

The ground
sloped down from
the jungle into a
huge crater. In its
centre stood the
yellow mountain Tommy had glimpsed
from the hatch of the Stardust. But
Tommy was more interested in the city
that shone in the sunlight at its foot.

If the robot spiders had been made in
a junk yard, thought Tommy, this must
be it. The city seemed to have been built
from bits and pieces of metal, some of
which seemed strangely familiar.

Tommy looked more closely, and
realized the building blocks were
sections of spaceships. A nose cone here,
tail fins there ...

So that was what had happened to
all the missing ships in Sector 13! They'd
been dragged to this planet by the

gravity beam and ended up as parts of
this city. But who was doing it?

Tommy saw something moving on the
floor of the crater. It was a line of robot
spiders, pulling something heavy behind
them. Tommy recognized it immediately.

It was the Stardust.

But Tommy didn't have time to think about what he was seeing. Suddenly, something cold and clammy gripped the back of his neck . . .

9
INTO JUNK CITY

The thing on Tommy's neck squeezed tighter, and tighter, and tighter. For a second he was frozen with fear. Then he swung round and knocked it off.

Tommy hardly dared to look at whatever horrible creature had attacked him. But when he did, he saw that it was a human hand. And like most hands, it was attached to a person.

"Dad!" he cried out. He threw his arms round Dad and hugged him. "I thought we'd never find you!"

Tommy let go and stepped backwards. Dad hadn't returned his hug or said anything. In fact, he was acting in a rather peculiar way.

"Are you all right, Dad?" Tommy said.

Dad was standing very still, his head cocked to one side and a blank look on his face.

You - will - come - with - me!

Tommy jumped back in surprise. Dad was talking in a strange voice.

"Keep your hair on, Dad," said Tommy. "Where are we going?"

"There – will – be – no – ar-gu-ment!" he said. "The – Varg – summons – you!"

Suddenly Tommy understood. Dad was being controlled by something! The thought made Tommy go cold all over.

Dad said no more. He walked off, heading down the slope. Tommy scrambled after him. He didn't have much choice. He knew now the key to what was going on *had* to be in Junk City, probably with this "Varg", whoever – or *whatever* – that might be.

"OK, Dad," said Tommy. "Take me to your leader!"

It was hard keeping up with Dad's long stride. By the time they were at the bottom of the crater, Tommy felt quite puffed. So he was glad when Dad stopped by a high metal wall and pressed a button. A square piece of the wall slid back, and Dad went into Junk City. Tommy followed close behind.

There were robot spiders everywhere, which made Tommy feel nervous. But he soon realized they weren't

taking any notice of them. After a
while, Tommy and Dad went round a
corner . . . and there was the Stardust, its
hatch wide open.

"Dad, look!" said Tommy.

But Dad didn't even give their
spaceship a glance. He kept walking

towards a large, black pyramid. Tommy
knew instantly this was where the evil
was coming from. He needed all his
courage to follow Dad through the
doorway.

"Tommy!" said a voice he recognized. "So they got you, too!"

It was Ada, and she didn't sound too well. She had been ripped out of the Stardust, along with a section of the control panel. Oddly enough, sitting on top of it was the mug that had disappeared with Dad.

"Ada!" said Tommy. "What have they done to you?"

"I'm not sure I can talk about it," said Ada with an electronic sniff. "Those robot creatures . . . Ugh!"

"Never mind, Ada," whispered Tommy. "I'll save us somehow. Have you seen Grandad? I'm sure they brought him here, too."

But Ada didn't get a chance to answer.

"Who speaks in the presence of the Varg?" roared a deep voice.

Tommy looked round – and found himself staring at the most terrifying thing he'd ever seen!

10 Alien Horror Story

Staring back at him was a creature that looked like a robot spider. But this was no robot. It was much, much bigger, and Tommy could see it breathing. He could smell it, too.

It sat at the heart of a gigantic, pulsing web. Connected to the web was a large machine with glowing, humming rings at the top. Grandad was standing

underneath them with his eyes shut.

"Leave him alone, you overgrown insect!" shouted Tommy.

"Silence, puny human!" hissed the creature. The web throbbed even harder. "No one speaks to the Varg like that and lives."

You don't frighten me!

Tommy pulled out his blaster.

"Stop him, slave!" screamed the Varg.

"Your – wish – is – my – command!" said Dad. He stepped forward and wrestled the blaster from Tommy's grip.

Just then the humming from the machine stopped, and Grandad opened his eyes. He walked over and stood next to Dad. Both of them looked lovingly up at the Varg.

"I see you've got a fan club," said Tommy, playing for time. "Er . . . tell me about yourself. I might want to join too."

Tommy didn't need to ask twice. The Varg obviously had two hobbies. One was talking about itself. The other seemed to be eating everything in sight.

It had gobbled up every animal on the planet years ago. Then a spaceship had landed. For the Varg, this was like being given a giant can of food. It had eaten the crew, and then come up with the idea of sending out an S O S to make other ships come.

The trick had worked, and the Varg had been living off spaceships ever since. It had built Junk City, the robot spiders and lots of other machines by using parts from the crashed spaceships. Tommy thought Ada's future didn't look too rosy.

"I get it now," he said at last. "If the S O S doesn't work, you can send meteor showers to force spaceships in the right direction. Then the gravity beam drags them down, and bingo – lunch is served."

"You are more intelligent than you seem," hissed the Varg.

"I'm glad you think so," said Tommy. "But there are a few things I still don't

Varg
slime

understand. Why were you so keen
to catch Grandad and not me? And
why . . . er, why . . . ?"

"You wonder why I did not eat you
all immediately?" said the Varg. "The

answer is simple. As soon as the one called Dad appeared on the planet, I knew he would be useful. And he has done much . . . *organizing* for me."

I'll bet that means tidying up, thought Tommy. The place did look pretty clean for the lair of an evil alien. Dad had probably even put that mug back on the control panel because it looked tidier there.

"But I knew the one called Grandad would be much more valuable," said the Varg. "That is why I made sure he was not destroyed in the crash. Already he has worked on the gravity beam to make it more powerful!"

Tommy had noticed a large machine on the other side of the web. On top of it was a shiny coil which pointed straight upwards.

"The only thing that old twit can make is trouble," said Ada.

The Varg ignored her. But she was right, thought Tommy. The Varg must be round the bend to let Grandad near one of its machines.

"So why did you send Dad to get me, then?" said Tommy.

"You harmed one of my robots," hissed the Varg. It started to move forward. Tommy suddenly began to feel very twitchy. "You seemed . . . dangerous."

Besides I grow... hungry

DinnerTime!

Tommy watched, horrified, as the Varg slowly moved across the web. Yellow slime poured from its mouth, and the smell became worse than ever. It was making some disgusting noises, too.

Tommy realized the creature was smacking its enormous lips at the prospect of a meal. Charming!

He knew it was no good trying to get through to Dad or Grandad. They were still standing in the same place, with the same stupid expressions on their faces.

There is No escape!

"That's what you think," said Tommy. "I'm off. So long, stinker! Catch me if you can!"

He turned to make a dash for the doorway. But he stopped before he'd even got half-way there.

A pair of large claws was coming through it.

They were attached to a robot spider,
one of the biggest Tommy had seen so
far. It was being followed by another,
and another, and another. Red beams
shot out of their eyes. This time they
were focused on Tommy.

"Oh dear," said Ada. "You do seem to be in a bit of a tight spot, Tommy. Does this mean you won't be able to save us now?"

"I'd have more chance with a bit of help, Ada," said Tommy, desperately looking round. "Haven't you got any ideas?"

"Did I mention there was another doorway over there?" said Ada. "It's to the right of that nasty great web thing."

"No, Ada," said Tommy. "You didn't."

There was no time to say anything else. The robot spiders were closing in on him, as was the Varg. It was beginning to move a little more quickly now, too.

"Resistance is useless!" it hissed.

Tommy ran over to the doorway. At the side was a button, like the one Dad had pressed when they came into Junk City. Tommy hit it. The door opened, and Tommy looked out.

Then he wished he hadn't.

The door led from the pyramid into an open space. But the way forward was blocked by a huge pile of bones. Most were alien, as far as Tommy could see, but some were definitely human.

Tommy turned round. The Varg was right behind him. He ducked past it and ran back to Ada, dodging robot spiders as he did so.

"I take it the other doorway wasn't much use," she said.

"Not really," said Tommy.

"Oh well," said Ada. "I suppose this is it, Tommy. I hope being that vile beast's dinner isn't *too* painful."

So do I!

Then Tommy remembered the mug
on the control panel. He picked it up
and threw it as
hard as he could. It
bounced harmlessly
off the Varg, hit some switches on the
gravity beam machine, and fell to the
ground with a clatter.

"You are brave,
puny human," said
the Varg. "But now
you must prepare
to die . . ."

Tommy wasn't listening. He was
watching the gravity beam machine
instead. It had
suddenly come alive
and was making
a terrible whining
sound. The coil
started spinning. It

slipped, and ended up pointing across, instead of upwards.

There was a loud bang. Then something like a bolt of blue lightning shot out of the coil . . .

grandad strikes Again

. . . and went straight into the body of the Varg.

The air crackled as the lightning got stronger. Soon smoke was coming off the Varg, and a hideous burning smell began to fill the pyramid. Yellow slime splatted against Tommy's spacesuit.

Tommy could hardly believe what was happening. The Varg seemed to be getting smaller.

It shrank, and
shrank, and shrank,
its voice getting
weaker, and weaker,
and weaker. At last,
the bolt of lightning
fizzled away and

Tommy could see nothing on the floor
but a tiny black dot. As he bent down to
look, it scuttled away.

It didn't get very far. Tommy glanced
up, and saw Dad striding towards him.
Without noticing, Dad trod on the Varg
and squashed it flat.

"Suffering
satellites,
Tommy," he said.
"What have you
done to your
spacesuit? I don't
know how many

times I've . . . told . . ."

Dad's voice slowed down as he began
to realize he was in a strange place.

"What's going on?" he said at last.
"Where *are* we?"

"It's a long story, Dad," said Tommy,
taking his arm.

Several days later, Tommy was sitting at the controls of the Stardust as it headed back to base. Dad was sitting next to him. On the screen, stars zoomed past.

"The new engines seem fine, thank goodness," said Dad. "I'm so glad we found some in Junk City. I thought we'd never get off that ghastly planet."

I wish some of us hadn't. You could have left that old idiot there. Playing with those robot spiders would have kept him happy for years!

"Now, now, Ada," said Dad. "I'm sure you don't mean that. Grandad's not that bad. I know we've really got Tommy to thank for saving us, but we might still be in the power of that awful creature if Grandad hadn't ruined its gravity machine."

Tommy smiled. Since their experiences on the green planet, Dad had been much nicer. He'd even let Grandad bring a robot spider back with him. And he hadn't told Tommy to tidy his cabin *once*.

"Anyway," Dad was saying, "where *is* Grandad?"

Just then the door opened and Grandad arrived. Dad and Tommy saw he was carrying the box that had started all the trouble. They both ducked.

"What's wrong with you two?" said Grandad, looking over his shoulder. "Oh, I see. But there's no need to worry about *this*. I've tried, but I just can't fix it."

"Now there's a surprise," muttered Ada.

Grandad took no notice. He simply turned and tossed the box into a corner, where it landed with a clang.

A ray of light shot out of the box.
There was a throbbing noise, then a
bang, and the light vanished. When the
smoke cleared, Tommy hardly dared to
look. But it was just as he feared.

Dad had disappeared.

"Er . . . sorry about that, Tommy,"
said Grandad.

Tommy was beginning to wish life in space would get boring once more. But somehow he didn't think it would.

TOMMY NINER

Look out for more
Tommy Niner space adventures:

TOMMY NINER AND
THE MYSTERY SPACESHIP

The crew of the Stardust are in big
trouble! They're flying into a lethal gas
cloud, and – YIKES! – that's Evil Zarella,
notorious space pirate, chasing them!

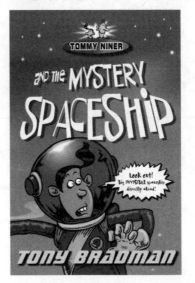